by the Sixth Grade Students of
Mt. Juliet Middle School
Mt. Juliet, Tennessee

WRITE TOGETHER PUBLISHING
Nashville, Tennessee

Published by Write Together Publishing ™ LLC.
www.writetogether.com

ISBN   1-931718-24-5 Paperback

Title: Change.
Author: Various.
Subject: Literary collections, poetry.

Project Coordinator:	Anne Barger
Cover Art:	Shelby Morris

For Write Together Publishing:

Publisher:	Paul Clere
Editor-in-Chief:	John D. Bauman
Art Director:	Bill Perkins
Publishing Representative:	Michael Pleasant

To publish a book for your school or non-profit organization that complements
your academic goals or values, vision and mission, please contact:

Write Together ™ Publishing
533 Inwood Dr.
Nashville, TN 37211

phone: 615-781-1518
fax: 520-223-4850
www.writetogether.com

Table of Contents

Mt. Juliet Middle School
1003 Woodridge Place
Mt. Juliet, TN 37122
615-754-6688
Fax 615-754-7566

Mike Gwaltney
Principal

Anne Barger
Asst. Principal

Dear Reader,

We celebrate the insight and thoughts our students have shared in the pages of *Change*. The middle school years are years of incredible change for young people, years in which their views of the world, and life are affected by their experiences.

We applaud our students' writing and we invite you to learn more about the middle school student through the thoughts they have shared in this book.

Enjoy!

Mike Gwaltney
Principal
Mt. Juliet Middle School

New Beginnings
Blake Billings

Nice place
Everybody is nice
We recently moved in

Being with new friends
Every day I go to school
Good people are the right people to be friends with
I like our house
Never late to school
Nobody home after school
I like school
No homework at our new school
Getting friends
School is fun here; everyone is nice

Different
Hillary Osborne

Days of school
Interesting new facts
Facing new friends
Famous new fashions
Eternal life with God
Running in gym
Everyone loves you
Nickname
Treating others with respect

A Recipe for a Life of New Beginnings
Bailey Primm

1 pound of growing up
1/2 cup of something you don't know
1 gallon of God
1 teaspoon of new parents
3/4 teaspoon of new babies
1 pint of attacks on America

Directions: Mix together thoroughly and you will have a life of new beginnings.

I'm Home Alone
Stephen Gilbert

I'm home alone and there's no doubt.
I'm home alone so now I can shout.

I'm home alone and now I can watch T.V.
I'm home alone so I can play in the R.V.

I'm home alone so let's make a mess.
I'm home alone so I can be a pest.

I'm home alone, uh oh, the doorknob is turning.
I'm no longer home alone and I'm in for some mourning.

New Beginnings
Brianna Benson

Our time is coming near.
I have no reason to fear.

I know it's getting closer to that time.
I can't wait to hear His trumpets chime

He'll take those who believe in one blink.
All the rest are left to sink.

So if you believe what I do, I'll see you up there.
Let's meet at His huge chair.

Kittens
Joseph Getsi

A litter of kittens was born today,
Three cheers for them, hip-hip-hooray!

A gray one, a black one, an orange one too,
Sleeping lazily with nothing to do.

Playing with a ball of yarn,
Going to explore a barn.

Dinner is soon to be coming now.
Then they're off to annoy a cow.

Back to sleep around their mother,
Don't forget the little brother.

New Beginnings
Caroline Sugg

Changes
New, unusual
Very different things
It is very weird
Different, cool
Changes

New Beginnings
Karen Kelly

Beginnings
Change, new
Many different things
Everyone goes through it
Difficult and hard
Cause changes
Beginnings

A Recipe for Moving
Jordan Buckelew

2 cups of excitement
1 cup of sadness
1 tablespoon of nerves
1/2 cup of old friends
1/2 cup of memories
1 teaspoon of tears
1/2 cup of new friends

Directions: Mix well. Try to avoid getting mixture too wet with any extra tears. If this happens, add extra excitement for a perfect new beginning!

New Beginnings
Jacob Addis

New beginnings
Start, go
Do your best
Believe in your dreams
Ignore your nightmares
Accelerate nonstop
New beginnings

New Beginnings
Molly Jackel

Baby
Funny, loud
Easily getting along
Has a cute smile
Has tiny feet
Stinky, odd
Baby

Return of the Lord
Carlee Smith

The Lord will return,
He'll take who believed.
Some will be rejoicing,
For He has finally come.
Others shall not
For they say it can't be.
For the ones who believed
Will forever be in God's eternal love!

New Beginnings
Dana Taylor

New schools
Everyone's happy
Writing in cursive

Boys are cuter
Exercising on weekends
Got ears pierced
Ike Freeman– new football player
New shoes
New dog
I'm getting older
New actions – tourist attack
Giving a hand and helping people
Smiles – world being nicer

Beginning
Danielle Cameron

You should remember September 11,
You should remember how frightening it was.
You should remember it was a beginning,
You should remember not a good one in fact.

New Beginnings
Samantha Sousa

New
Baby, house
Back to Massachusetts
Tennessee is really great
See my family
School, Dad
New

New Beginnings at School
Amanda Fultz

New beginnings at school are tough,
The people you meet can be rough.

You run around trying to find your next class.
While you are running, you and another kid crash.

So much homework, so little time till it's due.
If you don't do it, the teachers will be through with you.

This is why you have all my luck,
Because new beginnings at school are tough.

New Beginnings
Colton Shannon

Moving
Driving U-Hauls
A new school
A very new house
Needs new plants
New friends
Moving

New Beginnings
Kyle Madson

New
Fresh, nice
Willing to try
No time to procrastinate
Trying to do
Clean, cool
New

When Jesus Comes Back
Nikki Bates

When Jesus comes back, it'll be a sight!
When Jesus comes back, you'll see all of His might.

When Jesus comes back, He'll blow you away,
For He will amaze you each and every day.

He will take you away to a place with ease,
It will be a place where a blind man sees.

New Beginnings
Ashley Mitchell

When my friends were little, about two or three years of age, their mom and dad didn't take care of them. So their grandparents snuck in one night and took them. They still live with their grandparents, although they know where their mom is. Most new beginnings are bad and seem like they will last forever, but they won't. They will become part of your life.

New Friendships
Jolene Binkley

Having a new friendship is really cool,
You both can go splash in a pool,

Or just be chillin' in the park,
You both can read about Noah's ark.

Going to the theater to see a movie,
Having a new friendship is really groovy.

Having a new friendship is really awesome,
It can make you really blossom.

New Beginnings
Abigail Gray

New beginnings are real strong,
They could be short, they could be long.

Families here and families there,
That's what happens when families tear.

A new school isn't too bad,
So don't look so very sad.

I have a lot more to say,
But I have to start a brand new day.

Changes
Nikki Unland

Changes
Big, little
Can be good
Can be bad
I like changes
Do you?
Changes

New Beginnings
Jeremy Starks

One new beginning is starting middle school. I did not know if I would like it or not. I was very nervous on the first day. Everyone was nervous because it was their first day.

Moving
Stephanie Stegall

Some people think moving is sad,
And some people get really mad.

You may have to meet new friends,
But your friendships should never end.

New Beginnings

Kayla Meredith

On September 11, people were shocked and saddened
Over what had happened.

Four days after the attack,
We were planning to strike back.

People were buried under bunches of rubble.
We warned bin Laden he was in trouble.

Bin Laden said it was a holy war,
But how can it be holy when the world he tore?

We give our regards to those who helped
After the few days that we wept.

We've been fighting for our rights
Ever since that first night.

America, our country, is true,
That's why our colors are red, white, and blue.

Change
Tim Leppert

The changes of the season,
They happen without reasons.

The first season is spring,
Wonders it will bring.

The second is summer.
During this season some minds rot,
Some people get dumber,
A lot do not.

The third is fall.
This season is not a ball.
A lot of people seem fit,
But some people don't quite get it.

The last is winter.
The ice-cold winds feel like a splinter.
This season is cold.
The winter is bold.

My Changes
Brittany Patterson

I just lost my grandma about two months ago. She had breast cancer and couldn't breathe well. I just stood there as she died on September 3, 2001. Now that she is gone, she isn't hurting. I know today she is still looking down on my sister and me. She was the best grandma ever, always thinking about other people and not about herself.

Two days before she passed away, while in a wheelchair, she went to the mall to get toys for the playroom. I know she is happy and not in pain anymore. I miss her a lot. I would do anything to have her back. Now I have to start a new beginning without her.

School
Brittany Haley

School
Brand new
Lots of kids
Tons of new teachers
Being more responsible
No playground
School

New Beginnings
James Fleming

New life
Entirely new
Week

Baby
Establishment
Grandmas
Inner love
New house
New republic
Inner life
New government
Games
Security

Changes
Melody Gilbert

Changes
Fun, exciting
Happening every day
People sometimes don't like them
Some are neat
Bad, good
Changes

Friends
Chelsea Burroughs

Friends
Haley, Chelsea
Best friends forever
Happy at all times
Funny, weird, humorous
Always together
Friends

New Beginnings
Kyle Israel

One of my favorite new beginnings was moving here from Miami because I was little and I didn't like where we were living. I liked moving here because I was going to live in a big house and go to a good school. I made a lot of friends.

Changes
Brandi Griggs

Changes
New, old
Change is good
New beginnings
Changes

New Beginnings
Tim Ramsey

New school
Every day is a new day
Weddings

Babies
Episodes
Growing
Introduce
New friends
New house
Inventions
New year
Generation
Spring

Me Without You
Haley Burnett

A bell without a ding
Is like a bird without a wing.

A dog without a bark
Is like a day that's always dark.

A boat on dry land
Is like a person with just one hand.

A porcupine without spikes
Is like pedals without a bike.

Me without you
Is like a sneeze without a tissue.

New Beginnings

Faran Saeed

New school for me
Every holiday is joyful
Wonderful to have a family

Baby girl is born
End of a life
Gave a new life
Interesting day
Never will she be rude again
New teachers
In a new country
New friends
Good people caring for other people
Special are you

School

Molly Ross

School
Fun, cool
Meet new friends
Go to new school
Get good grades
New teachers
School

New Beginnings
Michael Conatser

Going to a new school
Is sort of cool.

You get to see new things
But you must get to class before the bell rings.

You get to meet new friends
And try out new trends.

You get new teachers, though some are mean,
But not very many that I have seen.

I think most people agree
A change is usually good for me.

Change
Adam Armstrong

Change can be good.
Change can be bad.

Change can make you mad.

When change gets worse,
Just look at a hearse
And be glad you're not in it.

When change gets bad,
Just be glad
That your family loves you.

When change gets hard,
Pull out some cards
And have fun.

I gotta go because I broke my toe,
And that's a change I'll have to get used to.

New Beginnings for School
Billy Ghumm

New year
Easy year
Work harder

Better food
Every day is a new beginning
Good teachers
It goes by fast
New school
No school on holidays
I meet new teachers
New friends
Get up early
School is fun

Friends
Nichole Wheeler

Friends
New, undiscovered
Meet, talk
A new friendship begins
Talk some more
Nice, kind
Friends

New Beginnings

Rachel Stocki

New beginnings all the time
Everyone striving to make it through the day
Worrying how New York is going to turn out

Begging and hoping that starting over was a good idea
Everyone trying to keep their goal true
Gaining more trust for myself
Isolating negativeness
Negative thoughts are left behind
Never thinking about stopping
I know I am going to make it
Not bad, but good beginnings
Going to start over better
Saying to myself I am going on the right track

Changes

T.J. Farrell

Changes
Getting older
Getting really smart
Starting a new school
Started getting taller
Started wrestling
Changes

New Beginnings
Chris Robertson

Neat and new
Everyone loves new things
Wonderful things happen

Beginnings are great
Everyone likes new beginnings
Great things always happen
I love new beginnings
New beginnings are wonderful
New beginnings can always happen
I think everyone enjoys new things
New beginnings are all around you
Good things are usually new
Special things are cool

Recipe for New Beginnings
C.J. Edmond

1 cup of new things
3 pounds of fun
4 teaspoons of school
5 drips of friends and family
6 pounds of all sorts of exciting things

Directions: Stir well. Mix with flour. Set oven for 375 degrees. Place mixture in oven and leave for 30 minutes. Enjoy!

New Beginnings
Nicolas DelPapa

I have had a lot of new beginnings such as a new school, new neighborhood, new house, new dogs, and new friends. Out of all these, I like my dog the most.

Change
Ira Chrisman

Change is sad,
Change is bad,
Change can be cool.
It feels like wool,
It is hard as wood,
And cool as a hood.
Change is awesome,
Like the Power Puff Girl, Blossom.

New Beginning
Meghann Hackett

New teachers
Everyone loves them
Whatever, some don't

Beginnings give chances
Everyone messes up sometimes
Giggling, smirking
I love to do them both
New beginnings give you chances
Not for you to waste
I try not to waste them but sometimes do
Now do you understand?
Great things come and there is nothing wrong with new

Beginnings
Alex Abdallah

Beginnings
New, things
School and friends
A new soccer team
Growing up fast
New teachers
Beginnings

New Beginning
Shawn Snyder

Night comes earlier
Easter
Winter

Bless the Lord Jesus
Ending the summer and starting the fall
Gifts on Christmas Day
I dress warmer for the winter
New presents
November
I open presents on Christmas Day
Nation begins again after September 11
God gave His son for a new beginning
September

New House
David Altizer

New house
No mouse
Pond with lazy ducks afloat
But it's too small for a boat
I have my own room
It's filled up with balloons
A fun place
To run and chase
New house

New Beginnings
Katelyn Woodward

New beginnings are hard
Everyone loves them though
When new beginnings come everyone is excited

Being born
Exciting
Getting a new brother or sister
In some cases new beginnings are bad
New stuff to explore
New things are sometimes weird
Interesting
New stuff is sometimes good
Getting new friends
So much fun

School
Shea Dehart

School
Big, cool
New to everyone
Very, very nice teachers
Place for learning
New beginning
School

A New Beginning
Raegan Cantrell

Maybe a divorce happened to you,
But don't be down and always blue.
A new beginning will come your way,
You just need to sit and pray.
A loss of a family member in days of last week,
A new beginning will come if you kiss another's cheek.
Sadness, broken heart, separation,
A new beginning will come with some preparations.
A new beginning is what everyone needs,
Something good for the soul to feed.
People looking far and near,
Not knowing that they will find fear.
A new beginning will come your way,
But it may come another day.

Change
Kristina Hannon

Everything around us changes every day, from the most drastic to the simplest of things. Changes may not be noticeable today. Someday I'll realize that change is the only way.

New Beginnings
Taylor Ervin

New beginnings are great
Like a very important date.
Some are good and some are bad,
Some can even make you sad.
Friends can be new beginnings,
Even when they take your pennies.

United Under the Flag

Andrew Jones

Bin Laden is very bad.
What he did was very sad.

Like the tragedy on December 7th,
We will never forget September 11th.

We try to help, we do our best,
While the government does the rest.

The American flag with red and white bands
Will keep us strong as united we stand.

We will keep our flag high, we will keep it real high.
For our country, we are willing to die.

He attacked America, he set off an alarm.
He hurt us bad, but we will do him much more harm.

His name is bin Laden, he thinks it's just a game.
We will hurt him so bad, he won't feel any pain.

I Thought I Was Organized
Brian Lawson

I thought I was organized until I opened my desk,
Until I fell and made a big mess.
I thought I was organized then I went into my room,
And when I opened the door it looked like a typhoon.
I thought I was organized until I did my work.,
Then I realized my dog ate it and I called him a jerk.
I thought I was organized until I went into the snow,
Then I found out I wasn't wearing any clothes.
I thought I was organized until I walked too far,
Then I figured that I lost my car.
I thought I was organized until I got out of bed,
When I stood up I hit my head.
I thought I was organized then I found some pennies,
Then I said I'm going to Denny's.
I thought I was organized until I was going to the mall,
But as I was leaving I had a telephone call.
I thought I was organized.

New Beginnings
Joey Mathias

My grandmother passed away just after I turned twelve on September 17. She died while eating breakfast. My grandfather was in the Air Force and he was tough, but that was the first time I saw him cry.

I rode to the funeral with him. I saw a tear in his eye. When we got there, I got out of the car and saw my whole family. They all started crying with him. The preacher told us some Bible verses and let two big men lower her casket into a hole. At that point I realized I would never see her again.

When I got home, I went to the corner of my room and cried until I fell asleep. That was a new beginning for me. I would have to live without my grandmother.

Four Seasons
Jonathon Baird

Fall, winter, spring, summer
Without four seasons life would be a bummer.

Winter, spring, summer, fall
Each is unique and I like them all.

Spring, summer, fall, winter
With each new season a new feeling I enter.

Summer, fall, winter, spring
Every new season has a new song to sing.

Osama bin Laden
Matthew Walczyk

You and your network destroyed two buildings,
Killed thousands of people,
And scared other people into not flying,
In turn, taking a serious toll on our economy.
Since we have been bombing you,
You've been hiding in caves like a coward.
When we find you,
We will seek revenge for all we have lost.

Change
Zachary Armstrong

Change is when you grow.
Change is when you gain weight.
Change is when something moves.
Change is when people die.
Change is what happened to New York.
Change happens to all.
Change happens in the fall.
Change happens in the rain.
Change happens when you get pain.
Change is when you get hair.
Change is when there's a fair.
That is all I have to say about change.

United We Stand
Sandi Caves

United we stand,
All over this land.

A nation under God,
Proud of who we are.

As the flag proudly waves,
I know we're going to be okay.

We can make it through,
No matter what they do.

As I sit here about to cry,
I wonder why and say good-bye.

Bob
Jake Rodefer

Bob likes to smoke,
Sometimes he chokes.
He wants to stop
Before he dead drops.
Now he's stopped and won't ever croak.

Change
Caleb Harris

Change is in the air everywhere you look. It happens to you and
me. It can be good, it can be bad. You don't know when it's happening, so don't feel sad.

If I Were in Charge
Taylor Hall

If I were in charge, I would only let change be good. I would keep
change away if it was going to hurt. I would try to keep everything
the same unless change is better. If I were in charge of change, that's
what I'd do.

Changes
Esi Amartey

C is for how cold it is.
H is for how hard life has become.
A is for how anthrax hurt people.
N is for how noble the U.S. is.
G is for how grand life is.
E is for how excellent I am.
S is for how strong we've become.

New Beginnings
Chelsea DeLoach

New
Earth
Wish

Birth
Erase what happened last
Go for the future, but still believe in the past
In Washington, D.C.
New York Trade Center
Now you can enter a new center
In New York
New world
Ground of new school
So many new things that happen

Change
Carter Lenard

Sixth grade comes after elementary.
We're now in middle school,
And we are always in a hurry.
This school has strict rules.
I live close to school,
Which is very cool.
I can't miss the bus,
So my mom won't have to fuss.

Change Is Everywhere
Josh Taylor

Change, change, change, it is a time for change
New school
New teachers
Everything has changed
Places to go, things to do
Change is everywhere
How about you?

Change
Mallory Washing

Change, change, change is sometimes good and sometimes bad.
For me, change is good and that's why I'm glad.
September 11th is not a good example.
Also it's not something you would like to sample.
Something else is making me have a fit.
A new school is more like it.
Change, change, change.

Accept Change
Alyssa Lauderdale

Sometimes change can be nice,
Or it could be like spice.
I have accepted it
Bit by bit.

Because change happens every day,
Or that's what people say.
And it's true,
So you can too.
Accept change.

First Day of School
Bailey Lester

When I went to school,
I wanted to stay in my pool.
It didn't work out,
So I had to shout.
School is a pain.
So is change!

Change
Matt Collins

I wish change were easy.
I wish I could control change.
I wish you could move and still have the same friends.
I wish people did not die.
I wish change were easy.

Seasons
Jonnah Goode

The seasons change every year.
It makes each year so nice.
In the fall, leaves change colors.
In the summer, it is so hot.
In the spring, flowers are blooming.
In the winter, it is so cold.
That's what makes each year so fun.

Changes in Life
Cory Benson

Changes in life
Occur every day.
Changes happen
In so many ways.

Change
Heather Hortenstine

It's hard to change,
You have to rearrange.

Change is hard and takes time.
I'm having a hard time making this rhyme.

Change is hard to do
For me and you.

Change can be pleasant.
At your housewarming party you might get a present.

Bin Laden
Toni Barber

Bin Laden, bin Laden
You are so rotten.

Bin Laden, bin Laden
Our country stands free.

Bin Laden, bin Laden
We know you're guilty.

Bin Laden, bin Laden
You did a horrible crime.

Bin Laden, bin Laden
You will do the time.

Bin Laden, bin Laden
We will heal.

Bin Laden, bin Laden
We also kill.

Bin Laden, bin Laden
Our country stands free
For all of eternity.

Change
Robbie Phillips

Changes in the world
I thought I would never see.
September 11th changed everyone,
Even me!

New Beginnings
Robert McCulley

There are a lot of new beginnings such as the start of baseball, football, and soccer season. I like new beginnings. They are fun. There are a lot of new beginnings.

Change
Rachel Griffith

Change can be good or bad.
Having change can even make you sad.
Always changing here or there,
Never a doubt, never a care.
Growing up with change every day,
Every change matters in its own individual way.

Change Is Everywhere
Glenn Bunt

Change is here.
Change is there.
Change is everywhere.
Change is good.
Change is bad.
Change is how we live.
Change is why we die.
Change is everything.

Change
Brad Cochran

C is for change in our lives.
H is for the hurt that change causes.
A is for anger that comes with change.
N is for when no changes are happening.
G is for the good things that change can cause.
E is for everything change brings.

September 11, 2001
Daniel Jones

September 11 was a day of fright
When two airplanes drove into our towers.
We cleaned up the mess day and night
Because of the fools and cowards.
Now was a time to struggle and fight back.
We bombed all his bases in a boom and a crack.
Because of bin Laden, peoples' lives were at stake,
Because of the hatred to us he could make.
The sorrow of his crime will always remain
As the fire goes out from the debris from the rain.
For the American flag, the stripes and the stars,
We stand free together. Americans we are!

Change
Megan Read

Change can be good.
Change can be bad.
Sometimes change could
Not be understood.

Seasons Change
Travis Boyd

Seasons change and so do I.
Lives revolve, sometimes we cry.
Some changes are bad and some changes are good.
Some change is never understood.
But once the change comes it will never go away,
Or it may on another day.

Change
Jeff Engebretsen

Change is good. Change is bad.
Change is big. Change is small.
Change can happen to one and all.

Always Remember
Sarah Barnhart

It's sad it takes something like the terrorist attacks to bring people together. People die, families cry, my heart beats 100 miles an hour, to the grave I take a flower. With each breath I sigh at death and hope the innocent souls will rest.

Always remember September 11th.

Change
Joshua Atnip

Change is bad and sometimes good.
We are going through it right now,
It is bad.
People from another country are trying to take away our freedom.
That freedom was not free.
My grandpa was one of the thousands that fought for our freedom.
I'm glad that we won.
I hope we win this one.

Coming to School
Ryan Overstreet

We came to this school
Not knowing where to go.
It changed our lives in a big way.
We did not know where to go or what to look for,
But we will find our sooner or later.

Seasons

Austin Agee

The year begins
Spring comes
The sound of laughter
And birds overcome

Then summer arrives
The sun is shining in my eye
All I see
Is a clear blue sky

Fall is coming
Put your jack-o-lanterns out
On All Hallow's Eve
"Candy! Candy!" the kids shout!

All the Change in the World

Tucker Wilson

With all the change in the world,
We are busy like a beehive.
With all the change in the world,
We are busy like worker bees.
With all of the change in the world,
Everybody is changing.

Change
Lauren Bolus

Change is good, but it can be bad.
Bad change can hurt. Good change can heal.
The good change will help the bad either way.

Time and Changes
Rachel Baker

Change is something we cannot change.
It happens to you and me,
Sometimes faster than we see.
As we watch each day go by,
There's never ever the same exact sky.
And while Earth is changing fast,
Some people on it just look on past.
One day we are young and free,
Time moves on and soon we're too old to see.
Not a moment should we waste
For time and change will not wait.

Changes Happening

Brian Larson

Changes, they are happening everywhere,
At home, at school. Usually everyone cares.
With our hearts we unite together for
A bright sunny day and good weather.

Change Will Never Stop

Kristen Carver

Change isn't bad, change isn't wrong.
Change is fast without a task.
Change can never be still, it always moves.
There is nothing anyone can do.
Change is fast, it will never stop.
That is good, don't let it drop.

Change
Anthonisha Lancaster

I have changed, you have changed,
We have changed together.
Although the attack on September 11 was bad,
It has changed us from bad to good.
People are helping people.
Families have come back together.
That's a change for you and me.

Trees in Change
Weston Gray

Throughout the year and day by day,
Trees change in many a way.
In the spring they sprout new green leaves,
And their limbs sway gently in the breeze.
In June they've risen towards the sun
And provide cool shade till the day is done.
The crispness and colors of the fall
Bring light and joy to one and all.
By winter the branches are dead and bare,
The tree sleeps on without a care.
So as you see, it's not that strange
The way the trees go through this change.

Change
Clark McAdoo

Change can be good or bad,
Change can be happy or sad.

Change can be really great,
Change can also be fate.

Change can bring joy or fret,
But change isn't all bad, I'll bet!

September 11, 2001
Krystal M. Smith

The day of the crash, the day of the terror, the day of two buildings burning together. This day was September 11, 2001. Early that morning two planes crashed they into the World Trade buildings. This event will not be forgotten. When your grandkids and kids are asking what happened, I believe it will not be forgotten. Osama bin Laden, that evil man, will be punished for what he has done. The bombings of their country are for the best. Maybe it will teach them to turn in that man. A question that we all need to ask is, "Did this unite us closer together?" It united us closer, it certainly did. But the lives of many people were taken in surprise, especially the lives of the people who work every day risking their lives to make it safe for all people. In years to come, that day will live on. It will remind us of the way we united in a way never seen before. So respect our country whenever it calls.

Change
Eric Bush

Change is good,
Change is bad.

I hope I won't be that sad.

You can rap like this,
You can rap like that.

But poeming will never be the same.

Change Is Everywhere
Lauren Carlton

Change is everywhere.
We breathe it in the air.

You cannot run, you cannot hide.
It is sleeping by your side.

If it gets me from behind,
I will not mind.

If it has not got you yet,
It will, I bet.

So change, you see,
Is a part of me.

New Beginnings
Missy Olson

New beginnings can be scary,
Some good, some bad,
Or someone getting married.
When new beginnings come around,
Don't be sad with a frown.
Friends are caring and very funny,
Even when they take your honey.

Change
Caleb Knox

Change can be good, or it can be bad.
Have you recognized the change in people after September 11?
A person cannot change the past, but can help the future.
God will be with you during all the changes you may have.
Everybody will change sooner or later.

New Beginnings
Waylon Carey

New things happen
Everything changes
Waylon is happy

Babies are born
Exciting things happen
Getting older every day
Interesting changes
Nice people enter your life
Neighbors move away
It's not so easy
Grownups get old
Stepmoms or stepdads are coming

Change
Justin Mitchner

Change, change,
Change is here.
We'll never forget
How it was here.
People are changed
Because their family members
Were killed and ill.
People aren't as secure
As they were before,
Because they still have fear
That there is a lot more to hear.
But in the end we will bring defeat,
And they will retreat.

Do You Like Change?
Bradley Haynes

Do you like change?
I like change.
There is no range for change.

Change can make you glad.
Change can make you mad.

Change can be the best.
Change can be the worst.

It just depends on how you take it.

Change
Stephen Smith

Change is slow,
Change is fast.
Change will happen in the future,
And change has happened in the past.

It comes and goes,
It goes from your feet to your nose.
Change is here, change is there.
Change is just everywhere.

New Beginning
Kaitlyn Wood

My life changed forever when my little cousin was born. I was the second person he saw in *his* new beginning. It was a new beginning for me too because I was not the youngest in the family anymore. I still look back on our new beginning.

Change
Lacy Reed

Our country has come under lots of changes,
From sea to sea where it ranges.
The military is working day and night
To fight for a cause we know is right.

The evil ones have left us in shambles,
But our jet planes are ready to scramble.
Osama bin Laden and his Taliban
Will come to know, We are the Man.

Changes in Life
Paige Gober

Change is forever in life,
From boy to man,
From miss to wife.

Change is seeing our lives come,
Fall apart in an instant,
From peace to war,
From carefree to careful.

Change is going to new places,
From a place where you've spent six years,
To meeting new faces.

Change is forever in life,
From beginning to end,
From freedom to strife.
Change is life, never-ending!

Changes
Katie Kelly

Every day we see smiling faces
Of kids just like you and me.

Some may be happy and some may not be,
But sometimes we just have to believe.

Change is something we all go through
Whether we do or we don't want to.

Somewhere between the war and fighting
Some courage needs to be breathed.

Courage is not very hard to find.
Just remember to care and always be kind.

Though you may hate change and it may hate you back,
Love everyone whether red, white, blue, or black.

Especially in this terrible time right now,
Change is hard for everybody who cares.

So show the world that you have great range
And show it that you aren't afraid of change.

To the best teacher I ever had - Katie Kelly

Change Is Everywhere
Andy Ligon

Change, it's everywhere—in the trees, in our hearts, and even in our school. The leaves are falling from the trees, the Twin Towers were torn down, and it's a brand new school. Some people's hearts were changed because some of their relatives were killed in the bombing on September 11, 2001. But some people just want everyone to get over it, like my sister. But like me, I think people should stay sad if they want to. Change, it's everywhere.

Changes
Joshua Cotham

This year isn't the same as last.
That is why it is not going by as fast.

I like change in some ways.
It just depends on which day.

Change can make me glad,
Change can also make me mad.

The Day We Will Never Forget
Kacey Lane

The day we will never forget, September 11, 2001.
It changed our lives forever, always.
The day we will never forget, September 11, 2001.
We will grow strong and bold.
The day we will never forget, September 11, 2001.

Changes
Jenna Bussell

Change is good, change is bad.
Sometimes change makes you sad.

But just lift your head up high
And reach up for the sky

Because change cannot get you down
Even if your smile is a frown.

The only reason you can't do that
Is because you have to believe in yourself—and that's that.

New Beginnings
Miranda Edwards

New beginnings are never endings. When you enter a race, you speed up the pace. Always finding something new. Try to blend into a game.

Change
Jennifer Dahl

Change may be good.
Change may be bad.

Either way we bear with it,
So make the best of this time.

You will think back in twenty years
And see how the world has changed.

It may be hard through this terrible time.
Just remember, hold your head high.

The Importance of Change
Brandon Ogden

Change is an important thing. Without change, everything would be dull and boring. Change happens every day. Sometimes it's good, and sometimes it's bad. It happens to everyone and everything.

Change
Stephanie Manners

Change is something that happens
Whether welcomed or feared.
Sometimes change brings happiness
And other times it brings tears.

Believing it will work out
Is something we should do.
God will take it in His hands
And faith will see you through.

Change is a part of our lives
That cannot be erased,
For all the change in the world
Will come at its own pace.

Prayer can help us through tough times,
In times of woe and sorrow,
Yet nobody can predict
Changes of tomorrow.

For what happens to us now
We may not remember.

Change Is Different
Lauren Dyer

Change is different,
Some good, some bad.
We all live with change.
Change will make everything different,
Sometimes a little,
Sometimes a lot.

Change can make you scared,
It can also make you happy.
No matter how hard you try
You can't stop change.

Divided to United
Shayla Ortiz

Indians to Pilgrims
Slavery to freedom
Country towns to cities
Outhouses to bathrooms
Radios to TV's
Black and white to color
Records to CD's
Typewriters to computers
Paper dolls to Barbie dolls
Bikes to scooters
Straight leg jeans to bell-bottom jeans
Glasses to contacts
Window units to central air
Twin Towers to ashes
Divided Americans to United America

Change: to go from one phase to another.

Sometimes change is needed to make us
Realize our value to each other.

Country in Change
Molly Hagan

The change this country is going through
Was not anticipated by me or you.
Who knew we would go to war.
When you'd look up in the sky, you'd see planes soar.
No one thought we'd have to deal with this.
But we do, so you're gonna have to put up with it.

Change
Sarah Robinson

Change is everywhere
In the fall, and in the world

Trees turning different colors
From red to orange or yellow to brown

Four hijacked planes
Changed the world forever

From being a little baby to having children
Changing in age day by day

Change can be good or bad
You never know when change is coming

Change is with you all the time.

The Fairy
Megan Tamas

And the fairy came out of her flower
To set free her awesome power.
Family and friends dread, but I will not have fear,
Because harmony will ring through my ear.
She will do what is right and not wrong,
Because she'll sing her harmony song.
Then all will be healed
And there will be no war in the battlefield.
She will then go back in her flower,
With her awesome power.
Now there is but one change to be done,
After that there will be none.

Why You Should Change Your Toothbrushes
Kayla Brown

Icky, sticky, nasty stuff,
All stuck to your toothbrush.

We have to change them pretty often,
Or your teeth will turn brown and rotten.

On them there are a lot of germs,
Microscopes will help you watch them squirm.

There are all so many different kinds of brushes,
To get the perfect one, you shouldn't rush it.

So you have a handful of what-to-do's,
Which makes many ways for you to lose.

Change

Shannon Gardner

Change is new places.
Having change is fun.
A new experience is neat.
New things have an affect on people.
Giving things means change.
Everyone loves change.

Love

Monica Manshadi

Love is everywhere,
Up, down, all around!
Its on paper and
Also in books.
It is shown by people everywhere.
Love, love, everyone should love!

Recipe for Change
Katelyn Poteete

1/2 cup of growth
1/4 cup of patience
2 cups of friends, new and old
1 cup of new and nice teacher (may substitute with funny teachers)
2 tablespoons of stuck lockers
2/3 cup of extra lunch money
1 teaspoon of lost agendas

Directions: Mix a 1/2 cup of growth with a 1/4 cup of patience. Mix well, then add the 2 cups of friends, 1 cup of new, nice, or funny teachers, and sprinkle with 2 tablespoons of stuck lockers, and 1 teaspoon of lost agendas. Add 2/3 cup of extra lunch money. Bake in a huge middle school for 8 hours and serve when needed.

Change Is…
Gabi Lago

Change is…
Finding out that your parents are getting divorced,
Then waking up in the morning feeling hoarse,
Never feeling that familiar comfort again.
You feel yourself grasping the memories,
And you feel confused, like me, I felt stunned.
Then I felt like someone pierced my heart,
If I could have danced it would have been like art.
I felt sad. I wondered how they could do this to me.
Was I being punished? I did not see.
Could I have done something different
To make them change their minds?
I could plainly see there was nothing left for me.
There is nothing that time won't change.
Won't you please hang in there with me?
Don't you see?
We gotta fight for life!
We gotta live!

Change
Brent Johnson

Change is good.
Change is bad.
Change is food.
Change is sad.

Change is care.
Change is fun.
Change is fair.
Change is the sun.

Change Is What You Do
Allen Hinkle

Change is what you do.
    Change is not to a few.
Change is like tofu.
    Change is like some foods.
Change is like a cook.
    It may create a book.
Change is like a brain.
    It can't be trained.
Change is like the nation.
    It's our own creation.
Change is like when you explore.
    You don't know what for.
Change is like some friends
    Because it never ends.

Change
Zack Mora

The world changes from day to day
    And that is always good.
Life throws us curves
    But we can take whatever
    Is thrown at us.
That is what makes us strong
And able to deal with life.

Change Poem
Hailey Malugin

Change is your mom or dad remarrying.
Change is you've got to get used to him or her.
Change is a new sibling.
Change is you have to be responsible.
Change is you're growing up.
Change is America now fighting.

Change Is…
Kimberly Palmer

Change is having to carry two classes of books.
Change is our books are heavier.
Change is having our heavy book in our backpack for homework
And my back hurts now because my backpack is heavy.

Change
Nick Pugh

There once was a boy who needed a change, and he didn't know what to do. So, he told his mom, "Mom, I need a change." "Well," she said, "look within yourself, and find yourself a change." So the boy looked and looked, but he could not find anything. He tried changing his style, but that did not work. He changed his hair, but that didn't work either. He even tried being cooler, but that didn't even work.

His mom had been watching, and told him a story. "There once was a boy who tried too hard to change himself, so his mom told him a story and the boy decided that he…." "What about the ending?" said the boy impatiently. "Make it up," said the boy's mom. The boy thought for a moment. "Changing my style, clothes, hair, and even being cooler made me popular, but I wasn't happy. Wait a minute. I don't need to change myself at all."

So if you're listening or reading, be yourself, not something you aren't!

What Is Change...
Justin Gesar

Change is... moving to a different mattress, house, or tooth brush.
Change is...going to use lockers instead of using desks and cubbies.
Change is...growing up.
Change is...going from 11 to 12.
That's what change is.

Change Is....
Michelle Ravech

Change is everything.
No one can change everything,
No matter who they are,
Or who they think they are.
No one can change everything.

Hope
Becky Crook

Hope is like a bird never stopping in one place,
Always spreading seeds of hope everywhere.

Change
Aaron Pelfrey

Change of the leaves.
Hanging the Christmas lights.
Away from home.
Never standing still, always moving forward.
Gigantic flakes of snow on the ground melting.
Everything is changing every day everywhere.

Living Today
Emily Grimm

Living today is a miracle to some of those who do.
Living today is romance, generosity, drama, and books.
Living today is changes, dreams, acts, songs, and writers.
Living today gives birth, breathes, plants, eats, and teaches.

But a question I have to ask you, "Are you living today?"

Change
Dakota Fay Weatherford

Change, change is
Everywhere change
Change is always there
Change, change can
Sometimes care but
Change is always there

America
Steven Yates

America
Makes
Everyone
Rejoice
In
Celebration
And happiness

America makes everyone rejoice in celebration and happiness because on September 11, 2001 we stood tall. That is what our nation is all about.

Change
Sara Benson

Change is always in your life.
Sometimes it may be so bad you want to change things in your life.
But sometimes change might be good.
Sometimes you may not care, but you should.
Change just might take away your life,
But at least you're giving a sacrifice.
So just keep change – good or bad – in your mind.
You'll have fun all the time.

A Loved One Is Gone
Caitlin Gray

When a loved one is gone,
The tears come on.
He or she was a good one.
It was a lot of fun.
You see your family cry.
All you can think to say is, "Hi."
Something you might blurt,
But you know it will hurt.

Change
Jonathan Hollister

    Many things can change—the school you go to, the leaves on the trees or even yourself. Change can sometimes be a good thing. After the attack of September 11, 2001 peoples' lives began to change. Just about every single day, you can see the American flag. Don't dread change because change will always be there.

War
Shelby Barrett

I'm sad that we are in a war,
But I understand what it's for.
It's so that we can have our freedom,
To stand up for what we believe in.
I hope that we are on our way
To having world peace someday.

Recipe for Change
Derrick King

1/4 cup of new beginnings
1 cup of the past
a dash of the future
a sprinkle of hope
2 cups of happiness

Directions: Stir thoroughly for 5 hours. Bake for 40 minutes and share with the world.

Change
Brittney Moser

C is for coping with loss of family or friends.
H is for helping each other with problems.
A is for all getting along.
N is for never giving up.
G is for getting it together.
E is for enjoying every little thing.

People
Nina Hall

Personal
Everybody
Others
People
Life
Everyone

September 11, 2001

Bruce Orr

What Osama bin Laden did was bad.
His dirty deed made America sad.

Just like the tragedy on December 7th
America won't forget September 11th.

We may have been attacked,
But we will never get held back.

Osama bin Laden may be able to hide,
But he needs to remember he will die.

America will come out on top
And we will make Osama bin Laden drop

Because we are Americans.

It Was Just Another Day

Jessica Troccoli

It was just another day
Until the Towers went away.

People were screaming everywhere,
Others just watched in despair.

New York was going up in flames.
Osama bin Laden was to blame.

The Pentagon was damaged too,
Along with four airplanes, passengers, and crew.

In just one morning the whole world changed.
Our nation will never be the same.

Those who helped lost their lives.
With their families we sympathize.

Victims' families suffered too.
At half-mast we kept the red, white, and blue.

This terrible tragedy we shall weather
For it has brought our country together.

Change

Preston Hunt

Change can be sunny.
Change can be funny.
Change can happen every year.
Change can happen far and near.
Change can be weird.
Change can be feared.
Change can be mad.
Change can be glad.
Change can happen in cars.
Change can happen on Mars.
So don't go thinking change is all good,
Because its not, but it should.

Terrorist Attack

Paige Bradshaw

Oh, say can you see what the
Terrorists have destroyed?

They can destroy our towers and bridges,
But they can never destroy our love and dignity.

They say they'll win this war, but that's not true,
Because they don't know who they're fighting against.

They may have a big army,
But our love will beat any size army.

The only thing that they've done that we haven't beat,
But we will, is sending anthrax in letters.

Anthrax has threatened to kill many,
But that won't stop us.

Changes
Nick Jones

Changes are good and also bad,
Sometimes happy and sometimes sad.

Changes happen all through the world.
If changes are good, then life is a whirl.

Changes can make life good and make it bad.
If changes are bad, then don't get sad.

No Longer
Beth Botts

Gone within minutes
They stand no more,
Hit by a plane
And fell to the floor.
But by this tragedy, our nation is stronger,
Even though the Trade Towers stand no longer.

New Beginnings
Lauren Stephens

Sometimes you feel like you are going to sigh.
Sometimes you feel like you are going to say hi.
Sometimes you feel like you are going to smile.
Sometimes you feel like you are going to cry for a mile.
New beginnings can be good or bad.
But always remember the good times you once had.

Changing Moods
Kalea Temple

Yellow makes me feel free.
Pink looks like laughing children.
Orange is a bopping color.
Green clears the mind.
Purple is my favorite; it's energetic.
Brown reminds me of rich chocolate.
Red keeps me alert.
White gives me a peaceful feeling.
Blue is a relaxing color, a perfect way to end the day.

Change
Chaz Bledsoe

What is change?
Change is smaller lockers.
Change is new friends.
Change is having new teachers.
Change is harder work.
Change is having a lot of homework.
Change is having a new building.
Change is having seven classes.
Change is switching classes.
Change can be good
And change can be bad.

If I Were in Charge of the World
Asfian Saeed

If I were in charge of the world, I would tell people what to do and what to organize. They could name me "Emperor of the World." I would battle countries with my superior armies to bring peace and freedom to the world. I would have no slavery and would give homeless people what they desire. My first name is Asfian (Aus-fee-on), which means "king of half of the world!"

P.S. I don't want to be a king.

Going Through Changes
Michael Palmer

I go through change every night and day, from sun to moon and light to dark. We get older and grow from head to toe, happy to sad and mad to glad. Our skills improve as we get older. If we think we want something, but then see something else that we want more, we change our minds. Remember, change can be good and change can be bad. So when you change one beautiful day, don't worry about it. It happens each day in every way.

Autumn
Heather Tyree

The sky is blue, the grass is green.
The air smells good, it's crisp and clean.
The leaves turn soon to gold and red.
Then Autumn will show her pretty head.

Not Like Always
Jennifer Griggs

One day you wake up just like always. Do the same things just like always. Go to school just like always. For some reason it wasn't just like always. Everyone was really sad. Then I found out why. The World Trade Centers had been destroyed. Two planes had flown into the two Towers. I remember so many people died, so many families heart broken. That day made our lives change completely.

Changing Clothes
Ava Caulkins

First I put on a shirt,
Then I put on a skirt.

Second I put on one shoe,
Having no clue where the other one is.

Third I go to the restroom to look for my brush,
But all I find is my old cat, Lush.
Then I go back to my room
And see my brush next to my old cherry slush.

Fourth I get my backpack and go downstairs,
Out the door and into our car.

Changes
Tyler Carr

Changes
Happy
Attitude
New Friends
Grow
Excellence
Strive to do better

Changes in Life
Logan Collins

School has change when you switch classes.
Your eyes have change when you switch to glasses.

Your life changes when you move houses.
Now you won't have to see any mouses.

I moved in just last night.
It was on Halloween and my life is right.

I love my house and it's super big.
Last night I saw a kid with a big black wig.

Now I'm going to say good-bye.
Oh my goodness I think I'm going to cry.

What Is Change
Sara Shelton

Change is having a death in the family
Change is having a divorce
Change is lockers
Change is switching classes
Change is ending elementary school
Change is having Coke machines
Change is having to move away
Change is getting new teachers
Change is getting friends
Change is losing friends

There are all kinds of change.

Change
Ashley Hall

Changing classes
Having lockers
A new school
No recess
Getting to meet new people
Every day is a new beginning

Since the Attacks
Stephanie Laney

Since the attacks on America on September 11, 2001 our lives have changed forever. We have lost some of our freedom, but maybe we can have more faith in God now. We are sadder because of what happened, but we have to keep praying for things to get better. Hopefully, the changes we have prayed for will soon come true. But as we all know, our country will never be the same.

Change
Mandi Sauls

Change—change is everywhere.
Change—change in every glare.

Change—change is very fast,
Even though it might not last.

Change—change happens to me,
But sometimes I just cannot see.

You'll meet change from time to time,
And now it's time I end this rhyme.

New Beginnings
Kate Campbell

No recess
English
Worksheets

Boys
Equations
Going to half lockers
Interrogatives
New stuff
No fast food during lunch
ISS
New teachers
Going to five different classrooms
Spanish

Change Is All Around
Matt Hinson

Change is all around,
From the peaks of mountains to the ground.
Change can be something that you seek,
Even in a bird's beak.
Change is special for people everywhere,
Even to ones who just don't care.

Change Is...
Paul Jackson

Change is getting new friends.
Change is getting lockers.
Change is getting older.
Change is getting more privileges.
Change is in the weather.
Change is getting new friends.

Colors of Change
Kyle Kawzynski

Yellow
    The color of leaves turning.

Red, white, blue
    Colors of the flag, which mean much more to us now.

Green,
    The color of money to help fight terrorism.

Black,
    The color of darkness, may we make it smaller every day.

I Feel Change Coming

Chelsea Burch

I feel change coming.
Change comes in all forms.
Change is in your family
And in your friends.
Change is in school and in life.
Change is in everything!

My Colors

Daniel Mathews

Blue, the compassionate and brave.
Red, blood for the freedom that we gave.
White, the harmony and freedom that we have gained
Through our hard work and pain.
Change, the color of red, white, and blue.
Change, the color of opportunity for me and you.

What Is Change?
Lindsay McNally

It's when you make something different,
It's when you do something new,
It's what you do when you get older,
It's what a flower did if it grew.

It's one of those things that can be good or bad,
It's one of those things that may last forever,
It's something that you might not like at all,
It's something you might be extremely thankful for.

It's something that may never go back,
It's something that we call change!

Change
Leslie Myhand

Change is scary.
Change is sad.
Change is good.
Change is bad.
Change is weird.
Change is cool.
You're even changing while you're at school.

New City
Amy Solava

I used to live in West Chicago, Illinois, and there are many things different here than there. One thing is that up North, we didn't say, "y'all" and "fixin'." We say "you all" and "going to," so it's weird to me. Another change that happened when I moved was picking new friends. I had to ask questions to myself, like, "Should she be my friend, best friend, or not a friend at all?" It's hard. That's what change is.

World Changed
Charlie Brooks

The world has changed
Since September eleventh.
There is more security.
Muslims are being mistreated,
And there is a lot more patriotism.
Wait a second, what is it I hear?
It's a chant, "USA! USA! USA! USA!"
The flag still stands proud and tall.
God bless America, one and all!

Change
Mark Walter

Change happens all around the world,
It happens to all the boys and girls.

I've found that the only way to deal with it
Is to go with the flow without getting in a fit.

Change can be big and change can be small.
I've been through a lot, but not quite all.

I've been through brothers and sisters going away,
I've felt the feeling of wanting them to stay.

I've seen my sister get married to my brother-in-law.
I love him just as much, and I stand in awe.

I said good-bye to my brother going to college.
I really miss him, but I guess he needs his knowledge.

I've moved to other states, like here to Tennessee.
Moving from Indiana was really hard for me.

I've been through many changes, and they were hard for me,
But just go with the flow, just wait and see.

Bin
Matt Bowers

There once was an old man named Bin
Who was filled with a ton of sin.
He brought fright to our nation
Along with investigation.
Now we shall find him in his den.

Change
Jessie Blankenship

Change may be good.
Change may be bad.
Change may be happy.
Change may be sad.

Change may be short.
Change may take time.
But results will show up
Through obstacles you'll climb.

Change comes to everyone,
The young and the old,
The weak and the strong,
The scared and the bold.

What Is Change?
Daniel Smith

Change is something new.
Change is sometimes scary.
Change is often frequent.
Change is when you start all over.
Change is when you meet new people.
Change is going to happen no matter what.
Change is a new beginning.
That is change.

Our Turn
Zach Powell

Two planes crashed because of bin Laden.
He thought our spirits would have fallen.

The Taliban were also in on it.
Now we will do things they will never forget.

Anthrax is also part of this.
People have died that we will greatly miss.

They've tried to kill people many times.
Now we will get them for their crimes.

The Changing Seed
Collin Young

I put the seed in the ground and covered it with soil. It grows into a flower by water and sun as it keeps on moving. The flower dies, the seeds spread, then it starts all over again. That's one of the qualities of change.

Change
Lance Harrington

Change can be good or bad,
So don't let it make you very sad.
If you don't get very sad,
Then you should become very glad.

If you have to change,
You should like it.
So don't change your range
And you won't have to like it.

When you don't like it
You won't have to like it.
And your life can go on
The same as it was
Before I came along.

The Day America Changed
Tyler Pumphrey

The world today is uneasy and fearful,
Many Americans are grieving and tearful.
Our country is great and can withstand
Any kind of threat or demand.
We cherish our freedom and will not fall,
Because we are united, one and all.

We Remember

Is Change Good or Bad?
Lindsay Blackard

Is change good,
Or is it bad?

That's your decision.

Some people say it's happy,
But others say it's sad.

So what do you think?
Is it good or is it bad?

Dear Brother
Rachel Calkins

"Dear brother, I didn't mean to change your room,
I only swept it with a broom.
It took all my might and must
Just to clean off a little dust.
I also cleaned under your bed,
I think I found something dead."
"Hey, I like it, sis,
And my mommy won't dis."
"Well my only intention was to let you know
That change is good, and good to show."

Change
Kayla Johnson

Change is everywhere,
In our hearts, in the world,
And in our minds.
Change can be a good thing or a bad thing.
Change can be a sad thing or very enjoyable.
Just remember everything happens for a reason.

Changing Ways
Shelby Morris

I pledge allegiance to the flag every single day.
Now I pledge allegiance in a whole new way.
I used to pledge allegiance only worrying about what I'm wearing.
Now I pledge like it's the world, pledge because I'm really caring.
I used to think it was boring; it was very long.
Now I stand very tall and sing the beautiful song.
Every time I get scared, my friends say, "It's okay."
I know this is true because it's the great U.S.A!

Change Is Everywhere
Sarah Smith

Change, change, it's everywhere,
Over here and over there.

Don't be surprised if you see change
Because it's happening every day.

Halloween was yesterday,
Barely anyone was out to play.

Last year
Everyone was there.

This is change, that is change,
Everywhere and in every way.

Change
Adam Curtis

Change is necessary
Happening all the time
Anxious to see tomorrow
Nothing can avoid it
Going on for always
Eternal, everlasting

The World Changed
Andy Barton

We all saw the events of September 11th.
We all mourn for those who went to heaven.

After the airplanes hit the Twin Towers,
I saw families who lost a member giving flowers.

I hope the U.S. will be strong
So we can prove bin Laden wrong.

The whole world changed in one day.
Now everyone has started to pray.

The world changed!

Change
Jillian Conover

Change happens every day
    In its own way.

It can be something as little as a new pair of shoes
    Or even a new hairdo.

But a big change is going on
    And we've all got to be strong.

The whole world is changing fast
    Because of the terrorist attacks.

Two planes crashed into our World Trade Centers
    Making our nation examine its pleasures.

We are now at war with the Taliban
    And people are doing all they can.

But change is going to be here always
    It's never gonna go away.

Things Are Always Changing
Rebecca Sharpe

Things are always changing,
Just like you and me.
We started out as babies,
Then moved on up, you see.
Before you knew it, we were teens,
Driving our own car.
Soon we were young adults,
Playing golf and making par.
Finally getting older,
We had to retire.
The job was great and all,
But we got a little tired.
We talked with our grandchildren,
Telling them how much they've grown.
Got around to telling tips
For eating ice cream off a cone.
Life went by fast.
It seemed like a plan was written.
Actually it was.
God had one for us as long as we've been livin'.

Printed in the United States
4111